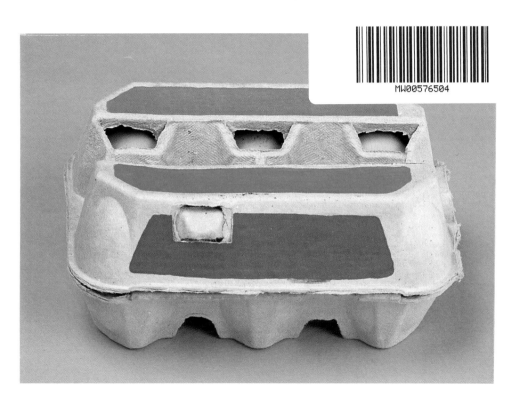

What's in the box?

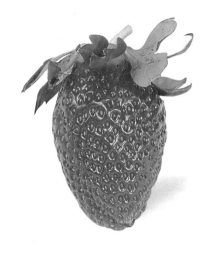

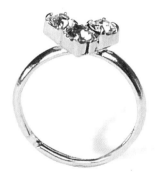

a strawberry   a ring

What's in the Box?

Nancy Ianni
Photographs by Malcolm Cross

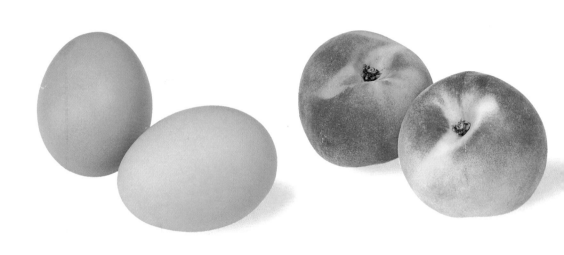

eggs   peaches

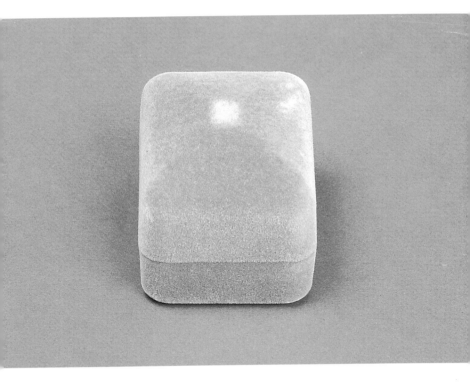

What's in the box?

a ring

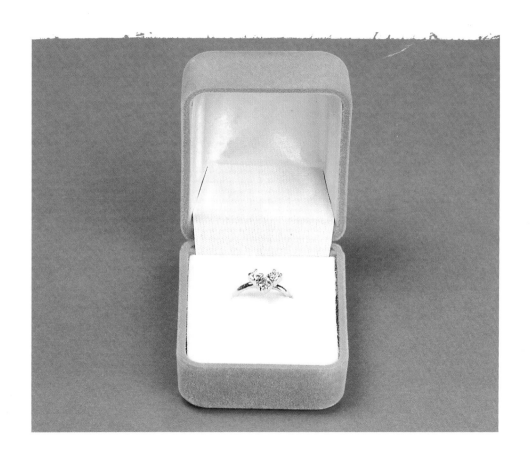

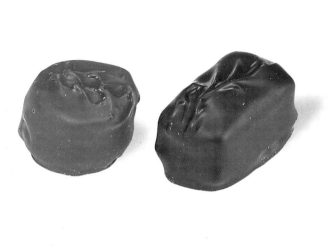 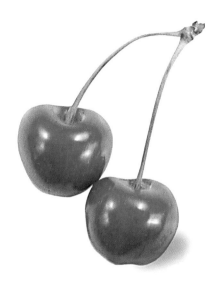

chocolates   cherries

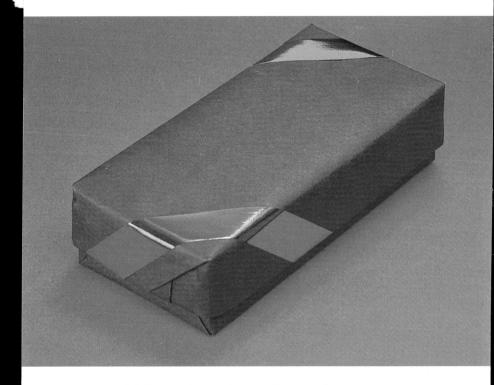

What's in the box?

chocolates

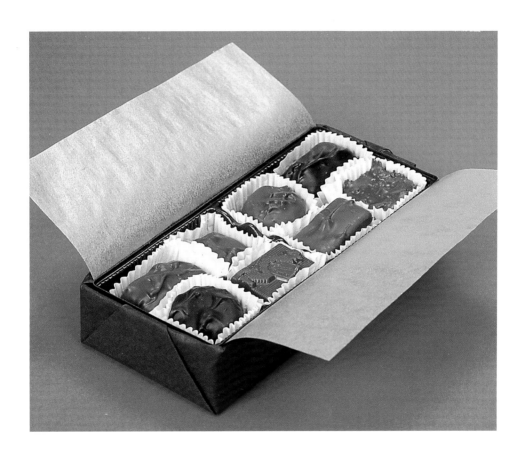

7

Index